I hope you enjoy reading my 3rd book. Always stand up for what you know is true.

Splash into Reading!

Stephanie Guzman

The Adventures of OLIVER the Clownfish: Sticky Fins

First Edition
Library of Congress Control Number: 2013903690
ISBN: 978-1-59664-008-5
Printed in the USA
In compliance with CPSIA
Code: JUV039220; JUVENILE FICTION/ Social Issues/Values& Virtues

Parenting Sandbar

Why do children steal?

A true understanding of the word stealing happens between the ages of 5–7. Most of the time younger children steal because they don't realize it is wrong to take things from others. As children get older the following are usually reasons for stealing:

- Lack of self control
- They want something they cannot have
- To be cool or fit in
- Because it is fun (thrill seeking)
- They want an adult's attention

Ways to handle stealing at home/school:

- Make it clear to your children that it is not okay to take something that doesn't belong to them
- Talk to your child to figure out why she/he stole
- Remind your child about the values your family lives by
- Have the child return the item and apologize
- If there are several occasions when stealing has occurred, it may be best to seek professional help.

More information can be found at www.familyeducation.com

Ten Things You May Not Know About the
Octopus

1. The Octopus lives only in oceans because it needs salt water.

2. An Octopus can get into very small spaces because it has no skeleton.

3. There are more than 300 different species of Octopi.

4. They are considered to be the most intelligent of all invertebrates.

5. An Octopus has very good eyesight but cannot hear.

6. Each Octopus has three hearts.

7. Should an Octopus lose an arm, it can grow another in its place.

8. Octopi can change their coloring to blend into the surroundings for protection.

9. The arms of the Octopus have suction cups on them that are very tiny and help them to pick up crabs, clams, snails, and small fish to eat.

10. The life span for an Octopus is very short. Most species live less than five years.

Information adapted from www.octopusworlds.com

Deep in the salty ocean there lived a happy, handsome clownfish named Oliver. Oliver loved his school, Fish Tale Elementary. His teacher, Ms. Stella the starfish, made everyone feel special.

"Good morning, class! Let's have a startastic day!" said Ms. Stella. "Does anyone have anything they would like to share today?"

"I do," said Paul the Puffer excitedly. "I brought some cool shells and rocks I found on my way to school. I really like this gold and purple shell the best."

"Those are really neat. I like your shiny sapphire stone," exclaimed Sally the Seahorse as she admired it.

"Thanks! Would you like to have it?" asked Paul.

Sally could hardly believe Paul's offer.

"I sure would," grinned Sally. "Thank you."

Sally carefully put the stone on the edge of her desk so that everyone could see it.

All the students in the class loved to look at Paul's precious trinkets, especially Ozzie the Octopus. Ozzie saw them sparkle like a star in the night sky. He wondered how cool they would look on his coral nightstand at home.

"Now where is my special teacher pointer?" wondered Ms. Stella as she tried to begin their reading lesson.

The class eagerly helped look for it, but couldn't find it anywhere.

Suddenly, Ozzie's voice cried out.

"Here it is, Ms. Stella!" said Ozzie hanging from the top of the coat closet.

Everyone laughed.

Ms. Stella read the class a story called
<u>The Finest Fish.</u>

After reading the story, she asked the class
to write about their favorite part.

"Write?" thought Oliver. "I am just no good
at writing, but I know my sparkly spiral
notepad will help."

Wanting to obey his teacher, Oliver went to
get out his notepad. "It's not here," Oliver
mumbled to himself in surprise. "What will I
do? I can't write down my thoughts without
my sparkly spiral notepad!"

Oliver raised his fin.

"Ms. Stella, my notepad is missing," cried
Oliver.

Once again, everyone searched for the
missing item, but couldn't find it anywhere.

"Here it is, Oliver," said Ozzie wiggling his
arm behind the coat closet.

"Thanks," said Oliver, relieved.

Meanwhile, Paul was also getting ready to write his favorite part in his notepad, but he couldn't find his favorite pencil with a shell eraser.

"Ms. Stella, I am missing my pencil," he called out to his teacher.

Again, everyone searched, but couldn't find it anywhere.

"Here it is, Paul," said Ozzie popping out from under the coat closet.

"Thanks," said Paul, looking at Ozzie a little suspiciously.

13

Whenever something was missing, Ozzie always found it. Oliver began to wonder why Ozzie always found the missing items. Oliver knew Ozzie liked being the center of attention. He had even been voted class clown in first grade.

Later that morning, the class was on their way to the cafeteria for lunch when Oliver remembered he had forgotten his lunchbox.

"Mrs. Stella, may I please go back to the classroom and get my lunchbox?" asked Oliver.

"Sure," said Mrs. Stella. "Hurry up."

Oliver quickly went back to the room and saw Ozzie was still there. He wondered why Ozzie had Sally's shiny sapphire stone in his hand. Then as Oliver walked further into the classroom he saw Ozzie putting the stone in his backpack.

Oliver was shocked, "Ozzie, what are you doing?" he demanded.

"I, uh ... forgot my lunch money and came back to get it," said Ozzie.

"No, I mean what are you doing with Sally's stone?" questioned Oliver.

"Oh, this thing? Just playing around ... this will be fun. When everyone comes back from lunch Sally will make a big deal about her stone being gone. You know she is such a drama queen. We will waste time from math because we have to look for it!" giggled Ozzie.

Oliver could hardly believe what he was hearing. "I don't think this is such a good idea. Have you been the one taking things from all of us?" Oliver asked.

"I sure have. With all of my arms I can take eight things at once," announced Ozzie as if he were proud of himself.

"Come on Oliver, you should try it!" urged Ozzie. "We will have a wild afternoon with more things missing."

Oliver thought for a moment as to whether he should have sticky fins. *Should I do it? I know we are doing fractions today in math and they are so hard...but I felt horrible when my notepad was missing. I can't do that to my friends*, he thought.

"Ozzie we shouldn't take things that don't belong to us even if it seems funny to you.
I was very upset when you took my notepad. I don't want our friends to feel that way," explained Oliver.

"You chicken Oliver?" coaxed Ozzie, getting ready to pick up someone else's stickers.

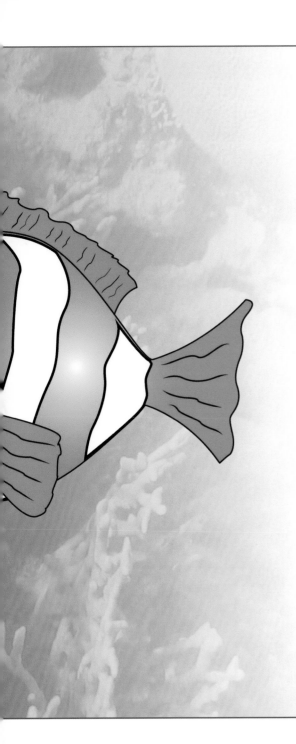

"How would you feel if someone took something that belonged to you?" Oliver asked.

"I would be upset of course ... but that would never happen to me," retorted Ozzie.

"Remember last week when we went on a field trip to the Rainforest of the Sea? You thought someone stole your super-slimy seaweed. It didn't feel good did it? But you forgot you put it in your pouch," said Oliver.

"Oh yeah," recalled Ozzie.

"Ozzie, it could happen to anyone. Please put Sally's stone back on her desk," pleaded Oliver.

"I guess you're right, Oliver. As much fun as I always have finding what is missing, it is not right," declared Ozzie while placing Sally's stone back on her desk. He was grateful for his friend's help in doing the right thing.

Oliver helped Ozzie learn that having sticky fins is not right. It's never a good idea to take things from others, no matter how much fun it might be.

About the Author

Stephanie Guzman is thrilled to share her third book in *The Adventures of Oliver the Clownfish* series. Through this book, she hopes to remind children that taking things from others is wrong and show how important it is to stand up for what you know is right.

Born in Maryland, Stephanie Guzman resides in Belcamp, MD with her husband Derick and daughter Katelyn. She received her Bachelor's degree in Early Childhood Education from the University of Delaware and her Master's degree in reading from Towson University. She recently became a National Board Certified Teacher. Stephanie works for Harford County Public Schools as a reading specialist.

Early in her teaching career she noticed not many books addressed the many character development issues important today. *The Adventures of Oliver the Clownfish: Invitation Slip-Up* was the first book and *The Adventures of Oliver the Clownfish: Acting Cool* was the second book in her series of inspiring children's books. If you have any ideas on what her next books should be about, feel free to email her at **stephanie@olivertheclownfish.com**.

Check for Understanding After Reading Sticky Fins

Ask your child to do the following to see if he/she understood the story:

1. Name some of the objects that went missing in the story.
2. How did Oliver going back to the classroom to get his lunchbox affect the events in the rest of the story?
3. What did Ozzie learn in this story?
4. Why did Ozzie change his mind about taking a friend's things and hiding them?
5. Why did Ozzie ask Oliver if he was chicken?